BRIDGE OVER SPOOKY WATER

A PARANORMAL WOMEN'S FICTION NOVELLA

MURKY MIDLIFE WATERS
BOOK FOUR

JB LASSALLE

MIGHTY OAK
PUBLISHING SERVICES

CHAPTER 1

The pirate ship arrived at the edge of the island just before dawn one week before Halloween, which was not cool with me.

I am *not* a morning person.

I was deep in the throes of a dream that had me squirming in my sheets. A man with dark hair and ridiculously strong hands made sure my every need was met. To my great surprise, I had a lot of needs. It was a recurring dream lately, and I both hated it and couldn't wait to get to sleep.

The shouting pulled me out of slumber. A thud shook the frames on my walls, and Bridge House gave an audible groan as though furious she had to wake up. Was Bridge House a woman? I didn't actually know, but the closer we got to the grand opening the more like a diva she became.

And the diva didn't like mornings either. Solidarity, girlfriend.

I stumbled out of bed and ripped open the balcony doors. The ship was massive—far too big to dock on the rocky shore of Bridge Island—and translucent. All of this should have surprised me, but at this point I'd seen too much. My primary thought was *huh, that's odd.*

A door opened portside. Or starboard side? A rope ladder

toppled out, and the din of chatter became a cacophony of music and cheers. Norbert was not yet at his perch, but I had no doubt he'd be unhappy that a massive vessel now nipped at his favorite sunning spot.

It shimmered in the rising sun, a clear indication of magic, but I still had to search my memory to see if I'd booked a party boat. I couldn't remember booking anything. Then again, I could barely remember the day before. We were one week from the grand opening, and I'd reached the forgetting-if-I-had-on-underwear stage of stress.

When the dinghies lowered and the inhabitants unloaded into them, my throat went dry.

A man stood in the middle of the ship, one booted foot propped on the edge like the mascot for that rum that always gave me a headache. He sported a tricorn hat and a mustache my Pop would envy. Deliciously dark curls fell to his chin. His body, long and slender, wore the unmistakable confidence of a captain.

He canted his head, catching my eyes across the distance and sending a shiver down my timbers. I gripped the balcony until my knuckles turned white, ignoring the sudden and irrational fear that Buford and his crew had flubbed its construction, and I was about to plummet to the ground. That was just my stomach, heaving itself up and down like it dangled from a bungee cord.

I'd seen his picture before. At museums and in books when I'd studied Louisiana history. I knew that cocky smile as well as the smiles I saw upon my friends' faces each day. But the portraits I'd seen reflected an intense, ugly man with pointed features and a greedy nature.

The man holding my stare was most definitely not ugly. He was younger and carefree and ruddy cheeked and oozed hedonism. I swallowed down on the lump in my throat, the gulp so audible I felt certain it traveled across the blissful fall breeze to reach him.

He tipped two fingers to his cap, offering me a grin that

puddled my knees. Against my will, my hand lifted in a goofy wave.

It was October, officially the month of pumpkin spice lattes (which I abhorred) and All Hallow's Eve (which I adored).

I was one week away from the grand opening of Bridge House.

And the ghost of the famed pirate Jean Lafitte was in my bay.

Great.

CHAPTER 2

$\mathcal{I}$ washed and dressed in record time, sprinting down the stairs long before my brain caught up with my body. Kitty waited at the foot, cup of coffee outstretched, three vivid ponytails flowing to her chin to meet her wry smile.

"We're making breakfast for the crew that docked. Invite them to the cafe."

Sizzling bacon enticed my ears, its delicious scent watering my mouth. All my senses, annoyingly alive before seven A.M. It should be criminal.

I grunted in acknowledgement, rushing to the door and bolting to the porch, where I slammed directly into a boulder of a man.

"Oof." Coffee drenched the front of my shirt and splattered into my eyes. I wiped them clear with a few furious blinks, only to meet Dimitri's equally furious glare upon me, his signature black tee a shade darker across the chest in a splash pattern that matched mine.

"I guess we can be glad you don't drink hot coffee." He wrung drips from the salt-and-pepper locks skimming his shoulders.

I stared into the mug, a small drip of liquid energy taunting me as the only remnants.

"Usually, I do." Kitty was no longer at the foot of the stairs but that didn't stop her snicker from reaching my ears. She'd known. Somehow, she'd known. And she hadn't warned me. "What are you doing here?"

"There's a pirate ship in the bay." Dimitri's brow furrowed like I was a madwoman. "Didn't you hear it?"

"Of course, I heard it. Do you think I'm up this early by choice?" I flicked my hair back, wincing at the spray of coffee creating a Rorschach on the wall behind me. The wood planks beneath my feet hitched, forcing me to stumble against the stain, then slammed back into place. I turned to glare at the damn house. "I would have cleaned it if you gave me five minutes."

"Misty, there is danger at your bay." Dimitri's voice edged toward impatience. It was a tone I was growing both used to and done with. In the six weeks since he'd claimed North Bridge, his emotions were a roller coaster I wanted off of. And yet, he kept me on the ride, showing up at different times of the day, offering help or hostility without being asked. Looking at me one minute like I was meat and he was starving and the next like I was a pest and he the exterminator.

He was going through some shit, and in his mind, I was to blame.

But it was too damn early, and I was too damn frazzled to offer Dimitri any sort of damn compassion. I whirled on him, ready to tell him to bug off so I could greet the freaking ghost pirate ship. My words died on my lips.

Jean Lafitte leaned on the porch railing, watching our standoff like a theater show created for his amusement. He'd removed the hat, and it dangled off two fingers. Laughter lit his chocolate brown eyes, which fixed on me and rooted me in place.

"On the contrary, old friend, it would appear danger has advanced from the bay and now resides at this lovely maid's doorstep."

Dimitri's shoulders lifted clean up to his ears and he turned to face the pirate. Lafitte was not translucent like his ship, and to his credit he met Dimitri's menace with no concern for his well-being. Who would win in a fight against a ghost and a troll? A lecherous little sliver of me hoped I was about to find out.

"I'm not your friend, Lafitte."

Lafitte mocked an arrow to his heart, though the mirth never lifted from his eyes. "You wound me, brother. Sure, and it's been too long since we reveled together, but I've a memory like a steel trap." He tapped a long finger to his temple "The story of our past reveals a different tale than the one escaping your demeanor, my dear companion."

He advanced the porch steps, and I had to admire his swagger. In my mind, troll crushed ghost, even if it was clear they'd met before. Or, if I believed the pirate on my doorstep, been pals. I had an image of Dimitri and Jean Lafitte, arms clasped across one another's shoulders, roaring with laughter and banging their tankards of rum in cheers as they pledged their undying friendship. It was such a vivid picture that a near-maniacal giggle escaped me.

They turned to me in unison, eyebrows disappearing under their dark hair. But the similarities stopped there. Dimitri's golden honey eyes, large and round, swam with harnessed emotion. Jean Lafitte's bid me welcome, roaming my body with an approval that lit my core on fire.

He stepped closer, lifting my arm and pressing thin lips to the back of my hand. Dimitri's body tensed, one hand squeezing into a fist. If Lafitte noticed, he paid it no heed.

"Greetings and salutations, madame. My name is Jean Lafitte, privateer and diplomat. My crew and I have come to honor the new mistress of Bridge Island and offer our services."

Oh, he was a charming one. *Thud, thud, thud* went my heart, deep in my chest. I shifted my gaze from Lafitte to Dimitri, capturing something in his eyes that gave me pause. Underneath the rage he wore like a shield was an undeniable flicker of fear.

Though my intuition told me Lafitte was no danger to me—not that I fully trusted it yet—one thing was clear. Dimitri was afraid of the pirate, or perhaps of the past he would bring to light. I still wasn't yet sure that I trusted the man who'd reportedly abandoned his mother on her deathbed and had needed far too much of a nudge from me to finally claim his birthright, but I definitely believed in his sense of danger.

An uneasy sickness settled in my stomach, but I had a duty to perform which included accepting the supernatural who found their way to me. And this sure as shit was supernatural.

"Welcome to Bridge Island, Jean Lafitte. As mistress of Bridge House, I'm pleased to invite you and your crew to a hearty breakfast at the cafe." I pasted a cordial smile across my face. "Why don't you bring them up, and we'll all break bread together."

CHAPTER 3

*T*hey swarmed into the cafe, and I took a chair near the corner to observe from a safe distance. Not safe enough, as a one-armed man balanced an empty glass and a full bottle between two fingers. With impressive dexterity, he slapped the glass on the table in front of me and poured from the bottle.

"Rum for the mistress," he said through a mouth that had smoked one too many cigarettes.

Though he tipped the bottle and held it, nothing poured into my glass. While the men drank, either from bottles or glasses of their own, they chomped from the bottomless plates Kitty managed to keep in front of them. I pretended to sip from my empty cup.

"You shouldn't drink that." Kitty shoved a breakfast burrito in front of me. My stomach tumbled at the sight of it.

"I don't want this." It was odd not to want to gobble something Kitty put in front of me, but the idea of eating brought bile to my mouth.

"I know you don't." She rolled her eyes, as if I'd said the sky was purple. "You need it."

I picked at it, wondering why the cafe seemed to tilt around me. By noon, the party showed no sign of ending. Occasionally, a foul-smelling swashbuckler tipped his drink to mine, still empty, and I nodded in gratitude and slugged back my invisible contents.

Jean Lafitte and a second man, older but similar in appearance, were at the heart of the festivities. They received claps on their shoulders and words of admiration. Lafitte dipped his head to me each time he caught me ogling, smiling as if he knew secrets I could only hope to understand.

For every glance from Lafitte I received, Dimitri's scowl took on a new level of dangerous. He'd perched himself along the railing, knocking aside any offers of food or drink. His arms were crossed, and his focus was intent on boring a hole through the rowdy pirates, who ignored him as they became mysteriously drunker on nothing.

There was a story there, and from the expression on Dimitri's face it would give me more insight into the mystery that was his past. We'd had good moments and bad in the past six weeks, but I still didn't feel like I knew him any better than I had before he claimed North Bridge.

I'd tried to connect to him. The gang at Illusion Square was using their resources to help me find Lucas, who seemed to have gone off the grid when he lost the battle with his brother. I'd had a plaque made to honor his mother and placed it on a bench that Buford helped me build. It overlooked North Bridge from a secluded little spot not far from Dimitri's cabin. Iris even helped me paint it in an attempt to mend their rift, though I'd had to convince her pink was not the best color choice.

But despite our regular drives and his constant hovering, he felt farther away from me than when we'd first met. And whether I wanted to have feelings for him or not, I didn't like it. Was he waiting for me to make a move? Or was he still processing his new powers? I couldn't tell.

In a moment of brazen stupidity, I decided now was the time to ask. I braced myself on my table to stand, eager to reach him and satisfy my curiosity. The cafe floor shifted, sending me careening toward Dimitri. I slammed into him, blinking to bring him into focus.

For a moment, something like desire darkened his features. Then he grimaced. "You have rum breath."

"That's not possible." I tried to point at my empty glass, found myself disoriented, and dropped my arm in defeat. "I'm not drinking anything."

His lips moved, but I couldn't make out his words over the sudden and intense squeal that raised birds from the treetops and sent them squawking into the sky. A blessed moment of silence took over the crowd, followed by a deafening roar.

Iris bounced on needle-thin heels at the steps to the patio, a sheen of joy in her eyes and hands clutched at her chest. She rushed forward to the cheers of the men, leaping into the arms of the older man near Jean Lafitte.

"Pierre, you rapscallion, where on earth have you been?" She lodged a noisy kiss on his cheek. He grabbed her waist and spun her around, a girlish titter escaping her lips as she was hoisted into the air.

"My lady, we've been barred entry until recently. Once we heard the call, we set out posthaste. Ah, but it's lovely to see my lass." He set her on the floor, his arm remaining around her waist, whispering words into her ear that made her cheeks flush.

"What call?" I stumbled away from Dimitri, bracing my hand on the doorway to the kitchen. "Who called you?"

Iris took me in, her gaze narrowing as I squinted to see her more clearly. With a disapproving gasp, she slapped at Pierre's chest. "Did you let her drink the rum?"

"Glasswasempty," I told her, my words a jumbled mess. "Ipretendedtodrinkisall."

"She's not one to hold her liquor, it would seem." Jean Lafitte's laugh warmed my insides. "Perhaps the good lady needs a bed."

Dimitri was on his feet before Lafitte had taken a full step, one arm extended to halt his forward progress, a look of pure warning sharpening his features. "You won't be taking her to bed, Lafitte. I will."

His neck darkened to a beet red at Lafitte's good natured chuckle. A sound I'd never heard myself make escaped my lips.

"Be off, the both of you. I've got this." Iris's hand was under my elbow, and she guided me to the island in the kitchen. The fete continued behind us, their songs filling the air.

"Yo ho, yo ho, a pirate's life for me," I sang along with a giggle.

"Be quiet and drink this." Iris shoved a mug of coffee into my hand.

"ThanksIwasthirsty." I lifted the mug to my mouth, struggling to find my lips. "Pierre seems nice."

"He's little more than mischief made flesh." Iris shook her head at Pierre, who winked at her through the window. A smile toyed her lips. "Damn fool, Misty. You can't accept anything from the supernatural."

"Why?" With each sip, my vision cleared, and the fog that had taken over my brain receded.

"You're connected to the house. The house is magic. So you are connected to magic." Iris clucked her tongue like an old mother hen, speaking in slow measures as if I were a young child trying to grasp nuclear physics. "Didn't Ruth explain this to you?"

"She's explained very little, actually." A dull headache pulsed behind my eyes. My mouth was bone dry. I took another sip. "Ghost rum gives me a human hangover. Awesome."

My stomach turned a somersault, taking the ground beneath me with it. I dashed to the kitchen sink, gripping the faucet as I retched. I let the precious water fill my mouth until I felt able to stand upright. Iris chucked a towel at my face.

"Ask Ruth what it's like to be mistress of Bridge House. You need to know how to do your job."

"I bet she doesn't know. She wasn't truly connected. Neither was my mom." That struck me, leaving a sinking feeling far more nauseating than the lingering sickness of a morning drinking.

Even after all I'd been through on the island, there was still so much I didn't know. There were huge gaps in my understanding of what it meant to be the mistress. Or Queen. Or whatever. I'd figured out the bed & breakfast part. I had my head wrapped around the mundane.

But not the waystation part. At best, I could spot magic, see the shape of it and those who possessed it. Why I could see it, though, and what to do about it, still eluded me

"I guess my grandmother was the last true mistress, but she died when I was five."

There was a haze of a memory of her, but not enough for me to grab onto. A warm smile, hair that flowed to her waist, a voice that brought the world to her doorstep.

A siren's song.

Who had she loved to embrace a life on land? What struggles did she face as mistress, or had it been easy for her? I heaved a sigh.

"I wish I could ask her."

"There's one here who can tell you." Iris's expression softened. She took the towel from my hand, pointing it toward the cafe doors.

As if aware we were talking about him, Jean Lafitte canted his head to me. For the first time, a hint of somberness calmed his features. An enigmatic smile crossed his face.

"He knew her?"

"He's known them all." Iris wrung the towel. "The House sends a pulse to the supernatural world, beckoning those who need it. The Lafittes were frequent visitors, both during its creation and every year after." Her expression turned wistful. "We haven't seen them since ..."

Her voice trailed. I waited for her to finish her thought, but she shook her head clear of it and offered me a false smile.

"Well, since it all fell apart. I imagine the bridge being unpassable made it difficult for them to return. But Jean Lafitte has welcomed every proper mistress of Bridge House in his, ahem, unique way."

13

"I'm not sure that's the kind of welcome I'm looking for." I shuddered, trying to suppress the little thrill that passed through me.

"Hey, don't knock it 'til you've tried it." Iris chuckled, as if she knew something I didn't. "Go upstairs and get some rest. I'll clean the sink, so Sam doesn't have a fit."

"A rest sounds nice. It's been a weird morning." A yawn snuck out of me. I trudged toward the stairs, stopping short as my phone buzzed in my pocket. I read the alert on the screen and slumped my shoulders. A rest would have to wait.

I had a job interview.

CHAPTER 4

"So, Max, tell me why you'd want this job."

I stared at the paper in front of me, a list of interview questions I'd downloaded after a quick online search, while the man sitting across from me scratched at his unruly auburn hair with long, dirty fingernails.

Man was a generous term. He couldn't have been more than twenty-five, with a patchy attempt at a beard and innocent hazel eyes that twinkled with amusement even though neither of us had told a joke. His fingers strummed a tune on the knee of his worn jeans.

I folded my hands on the table in an attempt to look professional. I hadn't conducted, or been on, an interview in a hot minute. The truth was that, unless he confessed to being a serial killer or kicking cats, I was going to give him the porter job. Thanks to Charley's tech-wiz roommate, we had a website bragging about the grand opening and bookings through the end of the year.

It was exciting, but it was also a lot of extra luggage and general support I would need. And while Dimitri insisted he didn't mind helping "until I found someone," and I appreciated the offer, he was still a mechanic in town who had his own responsibilities. And the new guardian of North Bridge. Plus, I wanted someone around who was less ... complicated.

And Max Reynolds, with his vintage Dr. John t-shirt and faded black Converse sneakers, was about as simple as they came.

"My gramps grew up in the city, and up until he died, he talked about Bridge Island. He told me there was something magical about it that I'd never understand until I visited." His voice held a tremor that twinged my heart. "He left me a tidy scholarship fund in his will, insisted I go to Tulane." His eyes brightened. "I wasn't sure about college, but he let me study whatever I wanted."

I gestured toward his t-shirt. "You chose music?"

He dipped his head in a vigorous nod. "Yes, ma'am. The city's music scene is top notch. All that history, all those ground-breaking musicians, and the vibe ..."

He leaned against the chair and closed his eyes, his face serene. That won me over. I knew the vibe of New Orleans well, and though I loved my little island and the home I was building here, there was nothing quite like the Crescent City.

His eyes snapped open. "Sorry. Got distracted. Anyway, Gramps said if I ever felt lost to go to Bridge Island. He said no one is ever lost here."

I leaned forward, a strange electricity lifting the hairs along my neck.

"Were you feeling lost, Max?"

He scratched behind his ear, his leg jiggling under the table.

"I'd say restless is more like it, ma'am. It took me some extra time, but I graduated. Had to honor Gramps's wishes. The vibe of the city lost its shine. I started to feel kinda closed in. Trapped." His gaze grew wistful again, and for a split second I could have sworn his jaw elongated. Just a touch. Then he shook his head so hard his cheeks wobbled and offered me his guileless grin.

"When I saw your ad online, everything just clicked into place, and I knew I had to apply. I'm a hard worker, ma'am, and I'm good at physical stuff. Stronger than I look."

I patted his hand, jolting at the rush of energy that nipped at my fingertips. I slanted my eyes at him, and sure enough the rough outline of the supernatural formed an aura around him. My stomach did a little flip. He was meant to be here.

"I'll be damned."

"You okay, ma'am?"

"Max, do me a favor and call me Misty." I rose, signifying the meeting was over. Max stared up at me. "You can stand, too. You've got the job."

"What?" He untangled long legs and jumped to massive feet, knocking his chair back. He turned to retrieve it, tripping over the carpet in the process.

I waited as he righted things, gnawing on the inside of my cheek to keep from laughing at the poor kid.

"Where are you staying, Max?"

"I got a place in Treater's Way." He grabbed my hand in both of his, pumping it like a rickety well handle. "Thank you so much, ma'am, I mean, Misty. I sure love this place, and I promise I'll do real good work."

I walked him to the door, smiling at his chatter while I gave him basic instructions. He scratched at his shaggy head one more time, then slung a beat-up guitar case over his shoulder, losing his foothold at the bottom stair and shooting me one last grin before he whistled his way toward South Bridge.

Behind me, a chuckle whispered in the breeze.

"I knew you'd approve," I told the house. "He's a gangly pup, but the guests will love him, and I have no doubt he'll be a hard worker." I turned and patted the door on my way inside.

"I wonder if he knows he's a werewolf."

CHAPTER 5

*L*ater that evening, I tapped one foot on the porch to make the swing rock back and forth while I watched the sun set over the bay. My head still ached from my supernatural bender, but the cool breeze of fall took the edge off the rest of my hangover. The pirates, having run out of things to sing about or eaten all our food, now corralled on the decks of their ship.

My siren song grumbled within. I longed for a swim in the bay and a visit with Norbert. With the season shifting, the world below the surface had evolved in ways that fascinated me. A bevy of new critters and plants were changing their patterns under water. It was a sight to behold, the way they eyed me with curiosity and a hint of fear, the way they swam alongside me. The way I felt like one of them, yet apart from them.

I had to admit it. Now that I wasn't fighting my nature, being a mermaid was cool.

But I couldn't get to Norbert, or shift into form, without approaching the ghost ship. After my interview with Max, I'd spent the rest of the afternoon avoiding them. Specifically, I'd spent the day not talking to Jean Lafitte, who'd roamed the house like a guest, poking at bookshelves and inspecting pictures in a way that felt anything but casual.

He had answers to questions I'd only begun to ask. And though I longed for more information, his presence left me with a sense of unease I couldn't define. I didn't know if I was reacting to Dimitri's ire over Jean Lafitte, or the knowing looks I'd found on the face of the self-proclaimed privateer every time I'd ventured near.

And yet, the inner whispers of my connection to the house scoffed at my cowardice. The pirates were here to welcome me, and they wouldn't leave until given permission by Bridge House's mistress. Which was apparently me.

The swing stopped in its tracks, frozen as if encased in ice. *Stop being ridiculous.*

I had to admit, it was a little disconcerting when Bridge House whispered to me. Before the renovation, it was just a feeling, a distant connection to something I couldn't quite define. During the renovation, boards lifted when I walked on them, or a wall inched itself closer. Now that Bridge House was fully renovated, the connection between us was not only strong, it was crystal clear.

Bridge House knew when I was being a coward. Bridge House knew what I wanted. Sometimes, Bridge House even knew what I hadn't realized yet.

Like the fact that the biggest reason I wasn't heading down to the shore was because I didn't want to upset Dimitri.

We'd been on eggshells for months, vacillating between the night we almost kissed and what I'd learned from Iris. I had questions for him, too, not just Lafitte. Like where had he gone before his mother died? Why had he really taken so long to claim North Bridge?

And why wouldn't he just kiss me and get it over with?

I was up here on the porch instead of down there in the water because I didn't want to alter the tenuous balance that kept us from either screaming in each other's faces or hopping into each other's beds.

That's not you anymore.

Creepy as it was to receive advice from a mystical house, she was right. The *old* Misty would walk on tiptoes to keep from making waves. She would do whatever she could to make sure there was no confrontation, and that the men in her life were happy.

Even at her own expense.

But that wasn't me anymore. I had a right to swim. To visit Norbert. And to meet with, and even flirt with, the hot-as-hell ghost pirate Jean Lafitte.

I was a supernatural badass. Sort of.

The swing tilted, forcing me to my fight.

"Fine. I'm going!" I pushed myself away and marched down to the shore.

CHAPTER 6

"*Took* you long enough."

Despite the sun disappearing under the horizon, Norbert remained perched on his sun rock. The ship was docked nearby, eerily devoid of voices or chatter. Did ghosts sleep? They drank. And ate. So it was possible.

"They sleep." Norbert grinned at me, baring his many sharp teeth. It was disconcerting when he did that, especially now that I'd seen him chop a snake in half with them and rip a tail from a mad troll's backside.

We'd been through some fun together since the start of summer.

I didn't reply or comment on how creepy it was that he'd known what I was thinking. I didn't even ask if he'd heard anything about Lucas. I strode directly to the water, trusting he would follow. I was much more confident in my transitions now, my tail shifting without so much as a thought.

With a ship full of leering pirates hovering over me, I wanted to wrap myself in a bag. Even if they weren't sleeping, whatever that meant for ghosts, I had no interest in drawing more attention to myself. Instead, I put on the bikini top I'd taken to carrying around. It's amazing how confident I'd become once I'd stopped showing my tatas to the trout.

Once my tail took form and Norbert slid alongside me, we sprinted beyond the channel, allowing my inner siren to guide us. She crooned in joy, and I gave myself into it, no longer feeling the tether of fear. There was nowhere my mermaid would take me that would lead me away from home. Of that, I was positive.

Norbert kept pace, bumping his body to my hip in companionship. The terror of almost losing him still lingered between us, and these moments when we left the island behind were one of my favorite parts of my new life. Once I began to tire out, we headed back to shore. Without communicating, we both lapped the ship to take it in.

Up close, it wasn't translucent, and it didn't take me long to realize that what I'd thought was a ghostly pallor was just my developing ability to spot the supernatural. Just like with Max earlier in the day, I could make out the residue of magic that formed its silhouette.

I moved closer, marveling at how the barnacles raised under my fingertips. A plank of wood left a splinter on my pinkie. I tapped it with my tail against the side, the sound not at all hollow or empty.

And if the sloop could be touched, then the inhabitants of it could be, too. Much like Iris had jumped into Pierre Lafitte's arms earlier, these spirits were corporeal. A shred of unease weaved through me. If they decided to do more than party, if they decided to raise real hell, they could be a threat to everything we were building on Bridge Island.

The undercurrent of fear in Dimitri's eyes came back to me. What did he know about the seemingly benign crew aboard? What did he know about their fearless and flirty leader?

"My, but it's a treat to watch a mermaid cut through water."

I'd been floating on my back, lost in thought when Jean Lafitte's voice shocked me out of my dark reverie. With a sputter that was anything but graceful, I dipped under water and swallowed a mouthful of moss.

He leaned over the stern, those intent brown eyes of his twinkling with the mirth I'd already gotten used to after only one day. Even with night completely fallen, the mischief of his expression reached me, causing another tumble in my stomach ... this one far less foreboding.

"Did anyone ever tell you it's not nice to spy on women?"

"Sure, and I've been admonished a time or two." He lifted his lips in a grin that displayed zero shame. "But when the woman is one such as yourself, mylady, I'm afraid my sense of wonder takes over."

I bit my lip to hold back my grin. He was a damn charming pirate. I held the silence between us. He lifted his eyebrows, tapping one finger in a display of patience.

"Get on with it, Misty. It's late and the water's cold." Norbert circled me, lifting his mouth above water to remind Lafitte he was there.

"You can't even feel cold water," I murmured. He nudged me with his tail. I heaved a dramatic sigh and lifted my voice. "Lafitte, I'm told you've welcomed all the mistresses of Bridge House. Given the unique way I found the island again, I'm at a loss for information about its past. If you have time for me, I'd love to, uh, pick your brain."

"My brain is yours for the picking, madame. Shall I come down?"

I wasn't ready for the conversation yet. It was late, and while I had covered my bits, I still felt exposed in the water. I'd rather have this conversation on solid ground. I wanted to think of the specific questions to ask.

And I was a chicken.

"I've hit my limit for the day." I swam closer to shore, letting my tail recede without exiting the water. "Would you join me for dinner at the house tomorrow?"

"'Twould be my pleasure, ma'am."

His smile spread from ear to ear in an expression far too pleased for a simple dinner request. His eyes gleamed under the moonlight. It was unsettling, the look, as if he'd won a grand prize, and my heart pulsed a beat harder in my chest.

I couldn't say why I knew, but at that moment, I was positive.

Jean Lafitte was up to something.

CHAPTER 7

$\mathcal{M}$ax was on my doorstep before I'd finished my first cup of coffee. I'd taken to working from my balcony in the mornings, and while I analyzed finances and planned events, he swept the floors outside, pruned flowers in the garden, and rearranged chairs in the cafe.

Lafitte and a few of his men roamed the grounds, so I stayed in the safety of my room longer than planned. I called Charley to check in, watching as they disappeared into the forest that lined the road to North Bridge.

By noon, any odds and ends I would have asked of Max were complete, and he surveyed the grounds like the steward of an old property. A steward with fleas, it would seem, as he frequently scratched behind one ear like a dog with mange. I joined him on the patio, following his gaze toward the trees now hiding the pirates.

"What do you see, Max?"

"A need to run, Ms. Misty." His eyes were round and hollow. His nose twitched as he took in the scents around him. "The path into the forest is overgrown. Difficult to follow unless you know your way around."

He blinked, clearing the fog from his gaze with a brisk shake of his head.

"Sorry, ma'am. I mean Misty. I don't know what came over me." He shifted from side to side, hopping from one foot to another as if about to take off in a sprint.

"It happens on the island, Max. Don't sweat it." I patted his shoulder, bracing myself as the electric sting of his inner magic shot through my arm. His outline was stronger today, already growing just from his proximity to Bridge House.

He was meant to be here. And he needed to be free outside.

"Hey, Max, what if I expanded your position a bit? We won't actually need a porter until guests start arriving in a few days. In the meantime, would you like to tame the grounds?" His mouth gaped open, and a soft yelp escaped his throat. "In fact, I've heard a rumor that somewhere near the edge of the island is a groundskeeper's cottage. Out that way."

I jutted my finger toward the path he'd been staring at like a long-lost lover.

"I can't say what condition it's in, but, in exchange for taking care of the lawn and maybe keeping the forest ... domesticated ... you're welcome to live there."

If his jaw dropped any lower, it was possible it would fall right off. The hope of a puppy being offered a treat lit his eyes.

"But I just started yesterday. You don't know me."

"I can picture it, though, and that's enough for me." I lifted one shoulder in a shrug. "Can't you see it, Max?"

I guided him closer to the forest. It wasn't much more than two miles deep, but it was lush. A few downed trees cluttered the raw beauty of it, and I could see how it might entice a wolf. A hint of a thatched roof beckoned just off the path.

"Buford, our construction manager, can help you fix it up if it's unlivable. Just tell him to touch base with me. And when our guests arrive, they will enjoy taking short trips around the island, maybe with picnic baskets provided by the cafe. An assortment of meats, cheeses, and crackers. Or romantic desserts and champagne."

I wandered forward, my toes touching the edge of the clearing, the vision of the forest shifting much like my tail when my siren sang.

"They'll follow the path you've created for them, laughing with glee as a rabbit scampers past or stopping in awe when a deer stops to drink from a puddle the recent rain created. They'll take their basket to the edge of the island, where it's nothing but water and nature and sky, and feel as if they're in another world instead of a short jaunt from New Orleans."

The trees shimmered as the view opened before me, as if by describing it I made it whole.

"On their way back, they'll stop by the groundskeeper's quaint little cottage, where our beloved Max will be strumming his guitar on the rocker he built. He'll dip his head to them with a wise smile, and they'll feel as if they've encountered something magical."

I sighed at the happiness of the moment, air rushing through me like I was falling in love for the first time. I hadn't gone into the forest since I was a young girl, but I could picture the scene, vivid and real as a memory. Max, but not quite Max, his hair longer and streaked with gray, his laughing eyes laced with cataracts, his fingers bumpy with arthritis.

"Of course, we'll have to restrict the path to daylight, so the wild can run free at night. Especially during a full moon."

For a moment, I'd forgotten Max was next to me. Then I realized what I'd said, and reality snapped back into place. The forest was once more overgrown, and the lanky kid panting beside me had no idea magic existed. Or that he was a werewolf. Not yet.

But he wasn't gazing at me like I was a madwoman. He could see the vision too, probably less clearly but nonetheless it called to him, much as the water called to me. A single tear marked a trail down his face. He swiped it away with the back of his hand.

"I think all that sounds amazing, ma'am. I don't know what

I've done to deserve it, but I'm sure grateful to be a part of what you've got planned here."

A thought tore through me, sudden and sure.

"Max, you said your grandfather visited the island?"

Max shuffled his feet through a pile of dust.

"He, uh, said he worked here once upon a time. When he was young." Max lifted his eyes to mine, something ancient reflected in them. "But between us, Ms. Misty, I don't think gramps was ever young."

CHAPTER 8

*a*unt Ruth's delighted titter and Sam's hearty bellow reached me on the porch before I entered the house. I turned the knob, which we never kept locked, and it wouldn't budge.

"Why are you mad?" Haughty anger radiated off the wood in waves that warmed my face. Whoever was inside, my diva of a building was not happy about it. I tapped down on the massive sigh building in my chest and put the tone I used to placate Charley with into my voice. "Whatever the problem is, I can't fix it from out here."

The door inched open, slamming shut inches from my nose when I stepped forward. Then it flipped open again, banging against the wall with a force that made me wince. I hesitated, just in case Bridge House decided it wasn't ready for me to enter, then slipped into the foyer. The door closed and latched behind me, thwacking my bottom along the way.

"You're kind of a bitch," I muttered to the wall. The lovely forest green paint Bridge House had finally let me apply dissipated before my eyes, replaced with bright daisy wallpaper. I grit my teeth, refusing to let a few walls get a rise out of me, and followed the laughter to the library.

A fold-out table had been nestled against the closest wall. It was one of those white ones with rickety legs, perfect for outdoor picnics and crawfish boils but not exactly an aesthetic match to the rustic charm of the room. The table was covered with a plastic blue tablecloth, fold lines criss-crossing at different angles as if it had been wadded into a ball and thrown into a closet.

On top of the table was an assortment of crudely made picture frames, adorned with misaligned and broken seashells. I picked one up, and the cardboard stand on the back bent under my hands. Some of the shells weren't actually shells but were rocks.

"What do you think? I made them myself!" I turned to the sitting area at the far side of the room, where Aunt Ruth and Sam held mischievous grins. My Pop stood, his ratty old ball cap circling in both hands, a look of pure hope on his face. "I finally did something with all those shells I've been collecting these years."

A thousand emotions whooshed through me at once. Pop hadn't been to Bridge Island in thirty-something years, not since I was twelve and my mother left us. He'd driven across North Bridge with me in tow and vowed never to return. Granted, it wasn't his fault I lost all my memories of the island, but we still hadn't reconciled the choice he made.

Last time I'd seen him, I'd hinted I knew I was a mermaid, though it wasn't something we'd stated outright. But then again, he'd written the check that allowed me to make renovations in the first place. And he was here. He'd driven back across the bridge to see me, to see the island, and he'd brought a peace offering.

Sort of.

I fiddled with the frame in my hands, wincing as one of the edges crumbled under my fingertips. These shells had sat under years of gunk on his bookshelf the whole of my life. With each fishing trip, he added to the collection. It hadn't been until I rediscovered the mysteries of the island that I'd understood them. He had remained connected to the place he lived with my mom through remnants of the water she disappeared into.

It struck me that he knew enough about the island to believe in magic. If he was shaken by the massive boat in the bay, I couldn't tell. I squinted my eyes at him, wondering if a magical outline would form, but none did. I was just squinting at Pop.

And why was Bridge House so upset about him being here? Was it because he'd taken me away, or was she worried I'd leave with him again? That would be silly. I was forty-seven years old, owned the house outright, and I'd claimed my legacy. Why would I be deterred from that by a few poorly made picture frames? After all ...

"... different colors if you like."

"Huh?" I blinked at Pop, pulling him back into focus. He chuckled at me.

"You still do that thing where you get lost in thought and forget people are talking to you?"

"I guess so." I shrugged, mostly to lift my shoulders to my ears and relieve some of the tension building there. "It's part of who I am."

"Misty Mae, I've always loved who you are."

My heart swelled at his declaration, but he jolted, as if it had come out unbidden. His eyes welled, and he covered what might have been a sob with a rough cough. "I was hoping you might sell them to your guests, the frames. I can make different colors, and maybe you can get more shells for me. You know ... newer ones, more intact."

He kicked a foot to the carpet. The house groaned. "And I'd sure love to take a look around at all the changes you've made."

I'd only ever seen my big, bold Pop look unsure of himself once before, and that had been the day we left. This sheepish man in front of me may as well have been a stranger.

But he was still my Pop, and I loved him with all my heart. Maybe understanding how to do the best with my future meant facing all the parts of my past, not just the most painful ones. I set the frame on the table, pretending not to notice that it didn't stand upright. I extended my hand.

"Let's go to the cafe and have lunch, Pop."

Kitty plopped a big bowl of jambalaya in front of Pop and a chicken salad in front of me. I didn't even know jambalaya was on the menu. He scooped a huge spoonful and shoveled it into his mouth, making happy Cajun noises as he chewed.

"That Sam sure knows what he's doing in there." He wiped rice off his mustache and dug back in. "Is the waitress new?"

"Kitty? No, she's ... been here a long time." I was feeling ten shades of awkward and had no idea how to broach the subject of magic. But even talking about that felt easier than asking why he'd taken me away or, more importantly, what he was doing back here. I picked at my salad, debating how to wade into the muddy waters of the conversation we were about to have.

"What is she?" Pop dropped his spoon with a clatter to chug at the sweet tea Kitty brought him.

"I ... what?" Considering how eloquently I'd shared my vision with Max earlier today, I was not doing a good job of talking. My tongue felt like it was twisted into a stupid knot, and the back of my throat was dry. "What are you asking?"

"You've got a mechanic troll who did a damn fine job of fixing up your mother's convertible, a half-golem making the best jambalaya I've ever had, and a mystical tree just a mile south of here." He swung his spoon as he talked, like he was conducting an orchestra of weird, then scraped the last of the food in his bowl. He tipped the bowl, a sad mutter escaping his lips when he found it empty.

Kitty returned with a fresh bowl. My stoic, surly Pop clapped his hands. He winked at her as she walked away, pressing her lips thin to keep from grinning. I sat back, abandoning my attempt to eat.

This was twice in as many days that Kitty had put something in front of me, and I didn't want it. I wondered what that was about. Meanwhile, Pop had talked about magic as casually as he had a car. This was the opening we needed to be honest with each other. I took a deep breath.

"She's a Kitsune, Pop, although I didn't know about Sam." I said, waiting until he'd shifted his eyes back to me before finishing. "And I'm a mermaid."

Pop's eyes filled again, and his lips trembled beneath his mustache.

"Part-mermaid, Misty. After all, I'm where you got your human side."

We held each other's eyes for what seemed like an eternity. A lump was forming in my throat, but it was different from when I was about to cry. My voice was rising, my siren wanted to come out, but not as a song. Not as a mermaid.

She just wanted a voice. So I gave it to her.

"Why did you tear me away from this? Why did you bury me inside Misty?"

I sounded different, my voice was deeper, with a gurgle I hadn't heard since I first discovered I had a tail. Pop's eyes went large with surprise, and he scanned my face in a way that told me I must look different. I turned to the cafe windows to catch my reflection. I still looked like me, but the outline of my tail filled the shadows under the table.

"Your mother only spoke to me this way once." Pop glanced around at the full tables, then leaned forward and dropped his voice to a whisper. "It was the day she said goodbye." His eyes were intense on me, like I'd never seen them before. "I was so scared that if I let you have a voice, you'd take Misty from me, too. I never for a moment thought you could live both lives."

Pop squeezed my hand, and as if that was enough, my siren curled into a ball and went to sleep. But it wasn't enough for me. The mermaid side may be simple and forgiving, but my human side raged at all I'd lost when I'd been taken away.

The house hummed in agreement. I swear, if I still had a period, and houses had periods, even our cycles would sync.

"Pop, I don't regret the life I lived in New Orleans. Daniel turned out different than I expected, but I have a beautiful daughter because of him, and Charley is thriving. But I didn't just lose my mother the day you took me across the bridge. I lost a chance to be who I was meant to. And a whole lot of people got hurt because of it."

Everything inside me was icky. I *hated* confrontation, and the last few months had been fraught with it. But at least that was clear cut. Lucas was bad. Iris was good. Norbert was Norbert. But this ... my Pop and I had been thick as thieves the whole of my life, and I'd put the hurt that haunted his chocolate eyes there with my words.

The few bites of salad I'd had turned sour in my mouth. An apology floated to the tip of my tongue, and I bit down on it so hard I tasted blood. I would not apologize for speaking my mind and expressing my emotions. No matter what. Not anymore.

"I know it, baby girl. And I'm right sorry for it." The tears he'd built finally broke through the dam, flooding down his cheeks in huge chunks. He ripped a yellow-stained handkerchief from the front pocket of his overalls and blew his nose, honking like an angry goose. "I'm so dang proud of you, Misty Mae. I didn't do right by you, but you're doing right by this island."

I don't think my Pop had ever said he was proud of me. In fact, I think this might have been the most words he'd ever said in one sitting. The sentiment, the tears, and his big strong hands melted my resolve.

"We both made mistakes, Pop." I let all my breath out, hoping to dissolve the rest of the ick. He blew his nose one more time and smiled before returning to his bowl.

"Damn good jambalaya."

I laughed. It was peace, tentative, but a good start. I could still sense the house's anxiety, though, and I knew it would take time for us to find normal again.

"Hey, Pop, I'll think about the frames. And I'll get you more seashells. Better ones." His smile grew, and my cheeks spread in return. "Now finish the bowl, and I'll take you on a tour of the house. She's a beauty, Pop."

He tapped his foot on the wooden planks of the deck, sweeping his toe from side-to-side as if rubbing the shoulder of an old friend.

"She always was. We were friends once."

A sad sense of longing washed through me, bringing with it a hint of a memory. Pop, alone in a room, chatting and laughing. He and the house had been friends. They'd understood one another. And he'd left her, too. And in her sadness and isolation, no one had taken care of her.

"I get it," I said, both to the house and to Pop. "We've all got a fresh start now. Maybe, with time, we can create a brighter future."

It was tenuous at best, the start of something but not enough to wipe away years of hurt. Still, I had hope that we'd find a path forward. I just had to figure out how.

CHAPTER 9

$\mathcal{I}$t had been a hot minute since I'd been on a date, and though I repeatedly reminded myself that dinner with Jean Lafitte was not, in fact, a real date my heart thudded in my chest like an adolescent girl's. I skipped my go-to athletic wear for a soft dress in a deep russet that reminded me of fall and made me feel confident. The color complimented my skin-tone and brought out the flecks of hazel in my eyes.

And sure, the dress was a touch low cut and clung to what little curves I had, but that didn't mean I was trying to get laid. I paired it with gold earrings that dangled in the blunt but stylish haircut Iris had fashioned for me. I wore a touch of mascara and a hint of lipstick. I looked like I'd tried ... but not too hard.

Aunt Ruth appeared in the doorway just as I was turning in the mirror to assess myself. She smiled in her way, like even the mundane was full of delight and wonder, then came to place an arm around my waist.

"You sure look pretty, Misty. All dolled up and whole the way you do."

Whole was not the look I'd been going for and though my first instinct was to question it, I realized it settled something within.

She was right. I looked whole. Not half mermaid and flopping in the water. Not half-human with shaggy hair and defeated eyes.

For the first time in longer than I could recall, maybe ever, the way I looked on the outside was a true reflection of how I felt inside. Even with questions about what it meant to care for Bridge House, I didn't doubt my ability to do it. I didn't feel frumpy or ugly, either.

Sure, I no longer had a twenty-year old's body. I was rounder in some places and softer in others. My eyes had little crow's feet at the edges, and my lips were thinner. But all those things didn't make me ugly. They didn't even make me imperfect.

How I looked was a reflection of the wear and tear of living a full life, and it was beautiful. Not always up to the expectations I'd set for myself when I was younger. Not always happy. But not always sad either.

I'd been a mother and a wife and a friend.

And I was a freaking mermaid.

All parts of the whole that was me. When I'd decided not to choose between my life on land and the world under water, I'd thought I'd always be torn in one direction or the other. But I wasn't.

Aunt Ruth was right. I was whole.

I appraised my appearance again, and the nerves I'd felt earlier fluttered away like dandelion seeds in a hurricane. I looked and felt good. For me. I hugged Aunt Ruth tight and headed down the stairs to get answers.

The nerves punched back when I approached the library, but just for a moment. Jean Lafitte made a dashing dinner partner, no doubt about that. He wore a tricorn cap and a long black coat. His white undershirt was a touch on the frilly side, but it revealed smooth muscles.

He was poking around an antique secretary in the corner. Sliding the drawers open with one finger while glancing over his shoulder. I cleared my throat, and he turned with a start.

Then his smile widened, his eyes alight with appreciation.

I had to admit, it felt nice to know I was wanted.

He lifted his cap and placed it across his chest with a small bow.

"Mylady, you are a vision. The brightest star in the night sky, to be sure."

What was it about the perfect compliment that wrapped around you like a warm embrace?

He gestured toward the cafe, and I followed. A delicate flowered tablecloth adorned one of the tables, and two tall white candles flickered under the lantern lights. Kitty scurried in from the kitchen. I felt awful that she was still there. I'd told both her and Sam I would cook, but they'd insisted on sticking around.

I peeked inside the glass doors and saw similar candles on the island. Sam's hair was combed, and he wore an unstained shirt. Kitty wasn't wearing her usual waitress clothes, either. She had on a black dress that grazed her thighs and scooped low on her chest. Her ponytails had satiny white ribbons weaved through them. Her lips gleamed with gloss.

I wasn't the only one on a date tonight.

Kitty cleared her throat, and I realized both she and Lafitte were watching me with expectation. Then I noticed something I'd never thought I'd see in my lifetime.

Kitty held a notepad and a pencil and was prepared to take our order.

My mouth dropped open.

"What ...?"

A blush rose across her cheeks, accenting the hints of pink under her tawny skin. She gnawed on her bottom lip, eyes downcast.

"I don't know what you want."

My mouth fell open wider. For two days, Kitty had been bringing me food I didn't want. Now she didn't know what to bring me at all. What was happening with us?

Lafitte waited with interested eyes as I considered. I didn't want Sam to cook something difficult, but I also had no idea what I wanted. I didn't even know if we had a menu.

"Uhm, is there any of the jambalaya that Pop had earlier left over?"

"Plenty."

"Sounds perfect!" Lafitte slammed his hand on the table, as though he'd reached some epic conclusion. "I'll have the same."

Kitty glanced between us, doubt shrouding her features, then nodded.

"Shall I pour wine while we await our food?"

I halted Lafitte's hand before he tipped the suspicious looking bottle toward my glass.

"No more ghost alcohol for me."

He chuckled, dipping the bottle further. A deep, red liquid swirled into my glass.

"Relax, mylady. 'Tis a gift from a bard in Grand Isle, given to my crew just last month. It's a harmless wine, if a little heady."

He clinked our glasses together in cheers, and I lifted the wine to my lips. The strong, tart scent of cherries set my mouth to watering. I took a tentative sip, a moan of satisfaction escaping me. This was more than a mere drink; it was an audacious burst of flavor, a symphony of taste that made me long for more.

It was as dangerously enticing as the man sitting across from me. With two fingers, I nudged my glass away from me and met Lafitte's charmed eyes.

"Call me Misty."

"As the mistress wishes," he said with a tip of his head.

"I haven't settled on mistress, either. I know that's what it's been called in the past but ..." I trailed off, fiddling with my napkin, unsure what it was I wanted to say. "I guess it's like that wine, the word mistress. Powerful and strong and rich and tempting. But it's not quite me."

Lafitte, to his credit, remained silent as I spoke. His expression grew more somber, and I appreciated the compassion that laced his voice. It was the first time I felt like he wasn't playing a game with me.

"Lady Talia was much the same when she arrived on this island."

Kitty appeared with our bowls and a thick, crusty loaf of bread. I tore off a chunk of it, enjoying the satisfying crunch as it broke away.

"Lady Talia was the first mistress?"

"Aye, and she built your house." Lafitte dove into his food with relish. "Born in Greece, I found her in Spain and dropped her at these shores myself." He winked at me, a lascivious grin showing me bits of food still in his teeth. "She'd have swum here, but I daresay I'm glad for the time I had with her."

"Did she say why? I mean why did she want to come here?"

"I know the why of her leaving. As for choosing this place? Put simply, mylady, the mystical energies here align. It's a potent location, as you've no doubt experienced. All manner of supernatural beings are drawn to it."

"But why?" I pushed my plate away after a few bites, frustration filling me. "Why are they drawn to it?"

"Few know the why of it." Lafitte dismissed my question as if it weren't important. "I knew a lovely nymph who said ley lines intersected just below the island. A fae once told me this was the location of a supernatural explosion. A dryad believed it was the convergence of the elements here, as they're all accounted for."

I thought about that last one. The island had a forest, heavy hurricane winds, and the heat of summer. It was surrounded by water. Had I ever swum underneath the island? I wondered what I would find down there.

"My, but it's a joy to watch your mind spin, Misty the mistress." Lafitte propped his chin on one hand and smiled at me. "Always in your head, as they say. Talia was much the same. In fact, of the five I've met, you are most like her."

"How so?"

"It's your mannerisms, I suppose." Lafitte gestured toward

me. "The way you move, with such an intriguing combination of self-assurance and trepidation. Always on the straddle of two worlds." He leaned forward, dropping his voice as if about to share a secret. "Kind-hearted Talia was carrying, you see, and wanted a safe space to raise her child ... whose father was human."

An ugly thought wormed through me, churning my stomach. "Were you the father?"

Lafitte's laugh filled the night.

"No, darling. You and I are not kin, and for that I'm grateful." He gave me a long look filled with promises I wasn't sure I wanted him to keep. "Talia was the last of your clan with two merfolk as parents. That is, until Marina."

That news was enough to encourage another sip of wine. I grabbed the glass with a trembling hand.

"My mother was a full mermaid?"

"Aye, and the call of the sea was a strong one because of it, I reckon."

An unexpected sympathy twinged in my heart. I'd had a litany of emotions surrounding the news my mother had been a mermaid and abandoned us: anger, confusion, abandonment. Even though I understood the pull of the sea, even when my own song had been at its loudest, I'd held onto disappointment in her that she'd chosen it over her family.

But this changed that. Had her siren screamed twice as loud? I couldn't imagine drowning that voice out, even for one day. My mother had done it for twelve years. Fresh tears blurred my vision of Lafitte. I blinked them away and leaned forward.

"Tell me about all of them. Please. Tell me all you know."

CHAPTER 10

*L*ater that night, after declining Lafitte's offer for company, I crawled into bed with a full mind and an empty stomach. Propping my head in my hands, I stared at the ceiling and let myself digest all the information he'd fed me.

Talia had been drawn to the island and built a home for herself and her daughter Cordelia. She was the reason it became a waystation, it would seem, as she wanted others to have a safe haven to discover themselves. It was here she'd nursed her broken heart after someone Lafitte had referred to as *that Irish rogue* broke her heart.

Given that Lafitte was much of a rogue himself, I wondered at how bad my great-great-grandfather must have been. Talia's daughter Cordelia hadn't spent much time on the island at all, and it seemed had chosen the mermaid's life early on. I was still unclear who my grandmother's father was. Lafitte had been cagey about that.

Cordelia returned with a daughter in tow, dropped her at Talia's feet, and swam away.

I wished I remembered more of Nerida, my grandmother. Especially now that I knew we had that in common. She'd been the last to truly love Bridge House, the last to choose it and raise her family here because she wanted to and not out of obligation.

Ruth, who it seemed was always meant to be landbound, and my mother were both placeholders. Waiting until I was old enough to make my own choices. And though I'd stumbled, pride swelled within me.

"We were meant for each other, weren't we?"

Took you long enough the house whispered into my heart, and we shared a chuckle.

The house was definitely a woman. She was all of us, my family line. She was a nurturer, a source of comfort, and a place to find the necessities of life: food, a bed, companionship. I didn't just own Bridge House. I was a part of it.

And being a part of something eased the pain of the many times I'd been rejected. That connection was enough to soothe the places in me I'd only begun to heal. While my Pop may not have made the best choices, he'd always accepted me. In fact, his acceptance had made him terrified to lose me.

It was time to stop focusing on the ones who hadn't been able to see me for who I am. I'd moved on from Daniel and, for the most part, my mother's rejection. This was where I belonged. That feeling of wholeness from earlier in the evening returned. Knowing who I was and what I was meant for had to be the key to helping others.

And yet, a thread of frustration still weaved through me. Lafitte had known my ancestors, and he'd known what they'd done at the waystation. But he couldn't tell me how. Maybe no one could, but Lafitte had not even tried.

Instead, he'd tried to get me out of my dress. Multiple times.

My mouth watered. I was hungry, but I couldn't figure out what for. The lingering scents of the evening still surrounded me. The earthy spices in the jambalaya. The sweet invitation of the Turks Cap we'd planted along the railing, opening their nightly bloom in offering. My vanilla lotion.

But Lafitte himself had carried no odor, no musk that

lingered after he was gone. In fact, he was somewhat of a blank canvas. A ghost of who he'd really been, literally and figuratively. While my face and body showed the signs of my life and experience, Lafitte was eternally in his youth. Forever on the brink of the lessons we learn along the way, with no hope of ever truly understanding them.

It rang hollow for me. Felt emptier than my stomach.

The idea of being young forever was an appealing one. But the reality was that eternal youth deprived us of all the things that kept us human. Things like screwing up and learning from those mistakes. Things like getting second chances.

I thought about my Pop's shoddy picture frames, and how beautiful they were. They were broken and imperfect and fragile.

And they came from a place of love.

Everybody should have a picture frame like that.

CHAPTER 11

*I*n four days, we would welcome our first guests to Bridge House. My stomach was twisted into a thousand tiny knots. My pulse throbbed in my throat. My feet were in constant fidget.

And yet ... I was bored.

Max was already working on clearing the forest. Every surface was polished. Sam and Kitty had the cafe running like a well-oiled machine. I knew everything I needed to know about the fancy system Charley's boyfriend had set up for me. I'd checked and double-checked the reservations.

Linens were fresh. Toiletries were stocked. Activities were prepared.

The only thing I didn't know was what to do with the supernatural that would soon appear on my doorstep. My evening with Lafitte had not given me the answers I'd hoped for. He still hovered in doorways or meandered the grounds. The crew showed no signs of sailing away, which left me frustrated and antsy.

I roamed the rooms, smiling at the seashell frames Pop had left on various shelves. The house, seemingly as restless as I was, lifted window shades and changed wall colors, presumably to get a rise out of me. Once she made my entire bedroom fluorescent green, I decided it was time to get fresh air, so I bolted from the house and headed to the shore.

"Why are you here in the middle of the day?" Norbert's greeting put my teeth on edge.

"What else am I going to do?" I snapped. "The house is ready, and she's being a brat. All I can do is wait for Halloween and just ... hope I know how to be a mistress." I shuddered at the word, still leaving a sour taste in my mouth.

I swear if he had had eyebrows they would have raised at me. "Wanna go for a swim?"

I plopped down beside him, tapping my toe in the dirt. I did. I really, really did want the freedom of the water, the uncomplicated ease of the other world, where instinct took over, and my siren knew just what to do.

"It's the middle of the day." I ran my fingers through the sand. "I can't just up and swim in the middle of the day."

Norbert shifted his massive body closer, resting his long jaw on my leg. It was heavy, enough weight to hold me to the ground. His teeth, sharp tipped and threatening, grazed my skin. He wouldn't speak from this position. If he did, that dangerous mouth of his would move, and he'd probably accidentally nip my knees off.

But the gesture brought tears to my eyes. What was wrong with me? Why did I feel like something horrible was about to happen, or like I was going to muck the entire process up?

"I've heard there are people who go through life just ... trusting themselves. Doing stuff they want and knowing it will turn out okay. With no inner dialogue. Being confident, like it's no big deal." I sighed and dropped my head to his. "Mostly men, I bet."

A deep rumble in Norbert's stomach served as his warm chuckle. In a few days' time, I wouldn't be able to do this anymore. Sit with Norbert half on my lap and chat with him while guests were in the house. I'd have to wait until they'd gone to bed to let my siren go free.

Everything had changed so much since I'd come to the island. It was all about to change again. And I had no idea if I could handle it.

"Fuck it." I nudged Norbert's snout, which only moved because he wanted it to, and dusted the beach off my butt. "Let's swim while we can."

The water was still cooler than summer, but midday there was a heat to it that wrapped itself around me. Instead of swimming away, we swam toward the bridge and frolicked. I practiced flips and turns, testing the strength of my tail and my growing flexibility.

"I should do more yoga," I laughed to Norbert, floating on my back. My fins slapped at the water, creating a rhythmic tap, tap, tap that soothed my already waning anxiety.

We watched the sun set from the water, drifting through the hours doing nothing. It was the first time I could remember letting myself just be in a long time. The first time I hadn't been torn between *this is nice* and *I should be doing something responsible.*

A few stars peaked out. North Bridge's iridescent sparkle brightened. I closed my eyes, not quite asleep but not fully awake.

Norbert drifted alongside me, a present source of comfort. My familiar.

And maybe because he was my familiar, and maybe because I was so comfortable, the thing I'd been holding onto all summer long slipped out of me.

"No matter how far I come, or how much I fight back, there's always a little voice inside me telling me I'm not enough. I know the house was meant for me, and I know I'm meant to be here."

Salty tears flowed to my lips, rolled down the side of my face, and plopped like tiny raindrops into the bay. A dam was bursting inside my heart, and, wrapped in my siren, I was powerless to stop it.

"But I don't think I'm equipped to handle the most important part. I don't really believe I can help anyone else, not with my whole heart, and I want that more than anything in the world."

A dragonfly danced on my tail, its wings humming as it flitted away. I let the tears I'd held onto all summer flow.

"If you believe that, you're not as smart as I thought."

The voice jolted me out of my melancholy reverie. I rolled to one side, searching the shore. We'd drifted further than I realized. Dimitri rested on the bench I'd built to honor his mother, one foot propped on the opposite knee. He approached me, a strange sort of anger swirling in the golden lava of his eyes. And though his voice was gruff, a rare compassion laced it.

"But I went through it, too. And you helped me get to the other side of it." He leaned toward the water and extended one hand. "Maybe I can return the favor."

CHAPTER 12

*T*he moon was right, his eyes were hooded, and his voice was honey. Every part of me itched to take his hand and let him lift me out of the water.

There was just one problem.

"I don't have clothes."

His grin wasn't all that different from the pirate's, but just for a moment. Then he trotted to the bench and picked up a canvas bag I hadn't noticed before. He dropped it on the shore in front of me. I furrowed my brow at him.

"I've taken to putting bags of clothes and a towel around the island for you at the different places you like to go when you swim. I'd brought this one down earlier." He grabbed at the back of his neck. "Just in case."

I had logical questions. Was he stealing my clothes or buying me new ones? Had he been waiting for me, or just enjoying the fall moon? One thing was for certain, the troll never ceased to surprise me, and like it or not, my heart danced in my ribcage at his words. I twirled my finger at him.

"Turn around."

With a sheepish grin, he turned his back to me. Norbert flicked his tail in my direction then drifted off in his soundless way. Which was good, because suddenly my senses were on fire. The sound of water falling off my body. The feel of pebbles under my wet feet. The scent of Dimitri after I dressed and brushed past him.

He sat next to me on the bench, and I took him in. Diesel and oak. Gravel and honey. Troll and ... good guy? No matter what happened in his past, he'd risen to the occasion when I needed him to. Multiple times. While Iris was steadfast that, ultimately, he'd let me down, I couldn't be sure. It seemed like the right time to find out.

"Where'd you go, Dimitri?"

He'd been staring out at the water as if I were still naked, but at my question, he snapped his head to me.

"I didn't mean for it to come out so blunt, I just can't keep dancing around it. Where were you when your mother died?"

"Iris told you I wasn't around?" His shoulders sagged, but his body stiffened next to me. When he responded again, bitterness coated his voice. "So that's why she hates me so much."

"It's not as simple as that." Usually, I blurt out whatever is on my tongue, but I took a moment to answer, thinking about how to word it properly. I didn't want to betray any of the conversations I'd had with Iris.

"Your mother spent time with you, alone, before she died. She asked you to claim North Bridge. Right?"

I waited for his curt nod and put a soothing hand on his knee. This would be a tough thing to say, and I wanted to be sure I didn't hurt him any more than I had to.

"Iris said you left, and your mother died crying that you weren't at her bedside." He pinched his eyes closed. "And that it destroyed Lucas. She said after that, he became more and more bitter. I think it ruined any real chance they had to be together, Dimitri."

Dimitri kept his eyes closed, but he nodded in agreement. Frustration rolled off him in waves, and I concentrated on watching the silhouette of his troll, still golden and lovely, even as he went through human pain. Then he covered my hand with his and gave it a squeeze.

"When my mom took me aside, she told me she was concerned that Lucas's intentions weren't pure enough for the bridge. She reminded me that everyone who has a purpose on the island must choose, and she was concerned he was choosing power over the good of others." His voice was rough with unshed tears. "She told me Lucas's father was the same, and that he broke her heart. Before then, she'd always said our fathers were just passing through. That's what happens on Bridge Island, right? It's part of how the island sustains itself, I guess. We never questioned it."

He sprang from the bench and paced a few minutes. Then, he whirled to face me, dragging fingers through his hair as if he aimed to rip it out.

"The only constant in my life had been my family. And Lucas was already pulling away from me. Now my mother was dying, and suddenly I was expected to take on this immense duty?! I was young and stupid and full of emotions. The only thing I'd ever been good at was fixing cars, and now she wanted me to harness some major power. It was too much." He plopped to the bench next to me. "I drove to New Orleans and went on a three-day bender that ended when I woke up on Jean Lafitte's ship outside Galveston."

"The same ship that's docked over there?" I pointed toward the general direction of Bridge House, as if either of us could see beyond the canopy of trees surrounding us.

"The very same." He let out a humorless chuckle. "I don't even remember meeting him, much less seeing a crew full of ghosts. Apparently, he really does haunt the Blacksmith."

I'd heard rumors about the bar growing up, but I'd avoided it. A small voice inside me whispered gratitude for my moment of good sense. I could barely handle ghost rum in my forties. I shuddered at the idea of drinking it in my twenties.

"Lafitte was cagey about helping me get back, and after a

time, I found out that Lucas offered him something to keep me away. He'd planned to claim the bridge while I was gone. He wasn't strong enough."

An uneasy chill slithered up my spine, and I looked over my shoulder as though we were being watched.

"What did Lucas offer him?"

"Don't know." Dimitri dropped his head to his hands. I ran my fingers along his back before I could think better of it. "Whatever it was, Lafitte never got it, which is why he told me about Lucas's plans and brought me back. Of course, by then ..."

It was as if Dimitri shrank under my hands. I lifted my head to the sky, where the full moon had reached high overhead. It blurred under my tears.

"By then she was gone." My voice broke as I said it. Dimitri rose again, and this time I stood with him, keeping my hand on him for comfort. He twisted out of my reach, as if he didn't deserve a soothing touch.

"Ruth was the only one who treated me the same when I came back. Iris and Lucas walked around with blame in their eyes. And North Bridge ... I can't explain it. It was like it hated me." I nodded at that. He probably had the same connection to it I had to the house. "After that, it became easier just to be angry. To act like a real troll."

He lifted his eyes to mine, and in that moment, I got lost in them. Those deep pools of gold, all that emotion, so much of everything.

"Then you changed that."

"I ... what?"

Dimitri stepped closer, bringing both of my hands to his lips.

"You hadn't been here a week, and you gave me your mother's car. You called me a fixer and trusted me to take care of it. My mother used to love that car; said it was a travesty what happened to it after your mom left. She always wanted to ride in it. You couldn't have known that at the time, but you gave me something I needed."

He grazed his finger along the side of my face, brushing back damp strands of hair, leaving a trail of tingles along my skin.

"You didn't even know me, yet you believed in me. And not just with the car. Why have you always known I would do the right thing, Misty, even when I didn't?"

I didn't know how to answer that, or if I could. My mouth was dry, and my stomach rumbled. Around us, the night was alive with the sounds of forest. All I heard was my heart, hammering its way through my chest.

"I did what my gut told me to." I licked my lips, tasting the bayou, wishing it was him. "I trusted my instincts."

Dimitri's smile dazzled me.

"And that's how I know you're not going to fail in your duties to Bridge House. Because when you follow your instincts, it helps others find the courage to trust theirs. It's how I knew I could finally overpower my brother, and how I was finally able to forgive myself enough to reconnect with North Bridge."

A thousand emotions played across his face, and a thousand emotions warred inside me. I wanted to argue with him, to insist that he'd done it himself all along and that it wasn't my instincts that had any part of that. It was just a spontaneous gesture. It was what I'd always done, often when I shouldn't have.

Why do you always act first, Misty? The memory of my ex-husband's voice rang through the night, as if he were standing beside me berating me. *Don't you ever think things through?!*

Sometimes I just know what to do, I would tell him in those moments, *I can't explain it.*

And I'd been doing it since I got back on the island. Giving Dimitri the car. Making an agreement with Lucas. Hiring Buford. Heck, even with Max I'd followed what my gut told me.

Each of those actions, done without thinking about whether they were the right choices. And each time, they'd been on the right path. Laughter bubbled up in my chest, lifting the weight of darkness I'd carried for far too long.

How could something as simple as trusting myself be so powerful?

"Sometimes, all we need to be ourselves is for someone else to accept us for who we are. I believe you will be an amazing ... whatever you want to call it ... for Bridge House." Dimitri wiped a stray tear from my cheek and cupped my chin. "If you can't trust yourself right now, I'll hold the space until you're ready, Misty. All you have to do is take the step in front of you. It'll lead you down the right path."

We were standing so close the heat of his body pressed against mine. His gaze filled my vision. I swam in those shining troll eyes of his. Eyes that saw me for who I was, imperfect and awkward and compulsive, yet still gazed at me as if I were a treasure.

I lifted to my toes, bringing our lips closer.

Had the moon become brighter? Were the trees rustling louder? Dimitri growled, long and low.

Or I thought it was Dimitri.

Then his body stiffened, his hands suddenly clawlike as they gripped my shoulders. He turned me, placing my back to his chest, one arm protective around me.

"We're not alone."

Behind the bench, the largest wolf I'd ever seen stalked us like prey. As its eyes met mine, it lifted its head and howled at the full moon.

CHAPTER 13

$\mathcal{I}$ knew those eyes, and it was the only thing that kept my heart from leaping out of my throat and heading for the hills. Even on all fours, his chest reached Dimitri's shoulders. It growled again, more uncertain than menacing. I knew the tone of that growl.

"Max?"

Dimitri's head swiveled to me. "You know the giant wolf, Misty?"

"I think this is the new porter. And the groundskeeper." My teeth were suddenly chattering so loudly it was hard to talk. If I were wrong, this would end really, really badly. I gripped Dimitri's outstretched arm and lowered it, edging myself forward.

"Max, is that you?"

The wolf blinked at me, recognition flailing in his eyes, and he let out a low whimper. His auburn fur shifted in the breeze. His nose twitched twice. Then he dropped to the ground and pawed furiously behind his ears. I sighed.

"Max, you definitely have fleas, bud. We'll have to get that taken care of." This poor kid. I hadn't had a chance to explain he was a werewolf. That transition must have been terrifying. I plopped to the ground, ignoring Dimitri's protest behind me. "I want you to know it's going to be okay. Can you hear me, Max?"

Max blinked at me. I held his stare, waiting to see if I reached him. If I couldn't, I'd have to trust that Dimitri's troll could subdue Max's wolf before he ripped my throat out. If I could, I might be able to help him. Wasn't this the thing I was supposed to do?

Dimitri was right. I had to trust my instincts.

"Max, I think your grandfather was a werewolf, and I think he was the groundskeeper here when Talia, my great-great grandmother, decided to create Bridge House."

He whimpered again, rubbing his neck along the grass. Dimitri dropped to the ground next to me. "Damn wolf needs a flea bath."

He was right. We'd have to do something about the fleas. But in the meantime, I wanted Max to feel settled and safe. I appreciated that Dimitri wasn't trying to throw brute force at the situation and was instead waiting by my side while I figured out what to do.

So, I took a moment to figure out what to do. What would I want if I woke up as a werewolf one day? I thought back to the morning I'd woken up with a mermaid's tail. I'd been confused and terrified. I'd wanted answers.

But not right away. First ... I'd wanted water.

"Max, the forest is yours."

Max's ears pricked in my direction, and he sat upright; a good boy ... waiting for his treat.

"Now and forever, the forest is yours to roam, provided you don't let guests see you. I mean ... unless the guests are supernatural, too, I guess. I don't know how that'll work, but we'll make the grounds off-limits after dark. We'll figure it out, bud. You keep the forest safe. You protect what roams it. You keep the cottage."

Max strode close, and beside me, Dimitri tensed. But earlier today a giant alligator had rested his head on my lap. And two minutes ago, I'd almost slipped a troll the tongue. So, all things considered, this was a typical occurrence.

Max flipped over, and I rubbed his belly. One leg kicked with joy, flooding me with a powerful surge of energy. He was pledging himself to me. To the island. And it fit, and in fitting, another piece of me locked into place.

I wanted to scritch behind Max's ears, but I held back. It was bad enough I'd rubbed his belly, and he had fleas. Dimitri lifted me to my feet, and Max pushed his head against Dimitri's thighs as if asking for more scratches.

Now that I was sure my life wasn't in danger, all the tension dissolved from my body. My head dropped back, and I laughed to the sky. It had been an emotional day, and I was amped up. I felt like dancing, like swimming, and like running through the forest with Max. Not that I could keep up.

I turned to Dimitri, who stroked Max's snout with one finger. This complicated, gruff, sexy-as-sin man had been by my side since I'd arrived at the island. Even when I didn't want him to be. A rush of emotions sent chills through me. I knew exactly how I wanted to burn off this new energy.

"Dimitri, why don't we—"

A cacophony of shouting reached us from the distant shore where Lafitte's ship was docked, followed by a piercing boom. In the sky, a ball of fire rose toward the stars. We sprinted toward the bay, reaching the levee just as a second shot pierced the sky.

Ghost or not, it shook debris loose from the ledge and reverberated through my body. The cannon was a ball of fire, brightening the night as it arched through the air and landed with a massive splash in the water.

THE MEN ON BOARD CHEERED, even as they loaded another. Though I shouted to them, they couldn't hear me. There was no way I could get their attention from here. I'd have to turn mermaid again to get closer to the ship, and that meant risking a cannon to the face.

MAX LIFTED his massive head to the moon and let out a long, distressed howl.

"IF ONE OF those hits the bridge, we're done for." I turned to Dimitri, eyes imploring. "So, I don't suppose you can, you know, do the troll thing and ...?"

I TRAILED OFF, gesturing along his body. Without a word, he strode to the ship, growing taller and golder and more naked with each step. Once he'd transformed, his head and chest rose above the ship, and I averted my eyes from his perfectly bronzed ass. Well, eventually I averted my eyes.

"As guardian of North Bridge, I command you to stop this nonsense. I will avenge any damage you cause!"

I got a little thrill from his statement, I had to admit. The guardian of North Bridge had spoken, and the raw power of it made me wiggle in my shorts.

"Apologies, mistress. 'Tis how they honor the full moon." Lafitte made his way down the levee, his cap in one hand. "I'll have them cease fire straight away." He eyed the werewolf pawing the ground next to me with an amused grin.

"Ah, young Max, I see you've taken after your grandfather! It's been too long since a proper wolf roamed this island. Mind you don't eat the fox, now, as she's one mighty fine waitress."

A third boom made me wince, chattering my teeth. Dimitri roared in anger, and the wolf beside me howled again. A hot, ugly rage filled me.

"Lafitte, that's enough from your crew. You're beginning to out-stay your welcome."

Lafitte's mustache twisted down as he feigned apology. I don't know how I hadn't seen through his charming facade before. Even as his face displayed sadness, his eyes were calculating.

"We'll set sail very soon, mylady."

He trotted toward the dinghy, then sailed out to his ship, shouting something at Dimitri that, for a moment, I was certain would get him pounded flat. Dimitri shook his head, waved at me, then plodded through the water toward North Bridge in full troll form.

And with my odds of having sex suddenly at zero, all my energy was zapped.

"Go on," I told Max. "Everything is well here, go enjoy your forest. Oh, Lafitte was right about the fox. Please don't eat Kitty."

He offered me one last adoring look, then bolted away from the scene.

It had been a long afternoon, and an even longer evening. The pirates weren't shooting cannons, but their partying would likely last the night, and I had no desire to be part of it. I turned away and trudged toward my bedroom.

As I tucked myself into bed, one thought shouted louder than the rest of the monkey chatter: Lafitte had been here in the house, alone, while we were distracted on the beach.

"What did he want?" I asked her.

And, either because she didn't know or didn't want to say, I received no answer.

CHAPTER 14

"Good morning, Jean Lafitte, privateer and diplomat. Might we have a word?"

I was up before seven again, and it still sucked. I dragged my tail along the water, flicking it into the air to grab his attention. He dangled his arms over the edge of his ship, drinking from a tankard and staring into the distance like he didn't know I was there.

I flicked my tail a shade harder. With a casual roam of my body, Lafitte finally let his eyes rest on mine. They lit with an appreciation that turned my stomach.

"Good morning, Misty the mistress, and what a fine one it is when a mermaid arrives portside to greet me. Have you come to invite me to another dinner?"

"Actually, no I'd prefer to talk here and now. That is, if you have time. Can you come down?"

"As the mistress wishes."

He disappeared for a moment, then reappeared with his tricorn cap atop his head and the same one-armed man who'd gotten me drunk when they first arrived. Together, they lowered a dinghy and rowed towards me.

My nerves hitched as I tread water waiting, but I held firm to my position. Even though he wasn't alone, they had no reason to show me malice. In the few days since they'd shot cannons under a full moon, they'd kept to themselves. Lafitte had remained on the ship during the day.

Kitty and Norbert reported that, although his brother Pierre had been seen slipping out and whistling as he jogged to Iris's cabin, Jean hadn't left the ship at night, either. And because I suspected whatever he was looking for was in Bridge House, I'd stayed close by.

He was either biding his time or waiting for a confrontation. Either way, I could no longer sit back to see what he would do. There was only one day until Halloween and the official grand re-opening of Bridge House.

It was time for this ship to sail.

Lafitte tipped his hat when he reached me, a smile playing upon his lips.

"Madame, as always, it's a pleasure to watch the wheels inside that lovely head of yours spin. I confess it makes a man wonder whether he might be so lucky as to be the target of those thoughts."

"As it happens, Lafitte, you are the target of my thoughts these days." I bit on the inside of my lip to keep from groaning. He was laying it on thick this morning. His hair was groomed, and his jacket pressed. Had he expected me?

His perfect face lifted into a smile, and it sent me back to the other night with Dimitri. Dimitri's face showed age. The skin on his neck was too red. His nose had a small bump along the bridge. His temples held gray. He had the same life marks I did.

I was right. Troll crushed ghost.

"I'm going to be blunt for the sake of time, as my first guests arrive in the morning. I'm still figuring out this waysta-tion thing, and I'm not sure all of them will be supernatural. I'm guessing the cafe has become the focal point of those drawn here. Either way, I'm concerned about the impact of, well, that."

I gestured toward his ship, and he dipped his head with a wry chuckle.

"Yes, mylady, I see your point." He met my eyes, for the first time dropping his facade and capturing my stare. "Am I to deduce that the mistress of Bridge House is asking us to leave?"

There was a challenge in his eyes, suddenly darker and rounder. Under the water, my tail shook as if I were fidgeting my foot beneath a table. I held it still and squared my shoulders. If he wanted to see how comfortable I was in my position, I would show him.

"I'll remind you I've asked you not to call me mistress, Jean Lafitte. This island and the House are my responsibility, and I believe we are safer without you and your crew docked here. So, yes, I'm telling you to leave." My voice had a tremor I didn't like, but adrenaline pulsed through me in waves. I lifted myself taller. "But first, there's something we need to discuss."

The slight twitch of his eyebrow was the only indication of surprise he gave me. From the moment we'd met, his posture had remained relaxed and confident. He had assumed that his knowledge of the island's history and my being thrown into the deep end gave him power over me.

But now, in my mermaid form and more certain of my ability to tackle my role, I was the one in power. And for a man like Lafitte, that couldn't sit well. He remained stone still in front of me, without a finger lifting or a toe tapping. And he looked at me as if he'd never seen me before.

"I'm listening, mistress."

I let the barb slide. I didn't want an enemy in Lafitte, and I certainly didn't want to fight his crew. There'd been nothing but battling since I'd arrived on the island. And knowing what I knew about Lucas and his history now, I had regrets about how we'd handled him. Even if he was conniving and dangerous, he shared one important trait with those of us who called Bridge Island home: part of him was human.

Lafitte had been human once.

"Dimitri mentioned that, long ago, Lucas made a bargain with you. He offered you a treasure to distract Dimitri while he attempted to take over North Bridge. Did you ever get that treasure?"

Water nipped at the edge of his tiny boat while he contemplated. I focused on keeping my breath even and hiding how nervous this interaction made me. Beside him, the one-armed pirate's eyes darted between us like we were volleying on a tennis court.

"Alas, no. Lucas provided me with a map that should have led to a most rare and precious gem. In exchange, the crew and I took Dimitri on an adventure far away from here. We followed the map and found nothing."

"What was the treasure?" Again, Lafitte paused, assessing me. I couldn't help but feel he was contemplating whether to lie to me. I decided to show my cards. "Lafitte, I've got no interest in being your enemy or stealing anything that is rightfully yours. I don't have any use for treasure. But you and I both know you don't intend to leave without it, that formally welcoming me was the guise you used to find what Lucas probably stole from you. Let's get this over with before Halloween. Okay?"

I extended my hand for him to shake. I didn't know much about pirates, not real ones, but I knew Lafitte's history. He was a bargain-maker and a treasure-seeker. At his core, Jean Lafitte was greedy.

Lafitte took my hand with a grin, then brought it to his lips.

"Misty of Bridge House, I believe you may be the best mistress the island's had." I slid my hand out of his palm, resisting the urge to wipe away the feel of his touch. "Talia's Star. A necklace of gold and pearl, inlaid with a jewel as pure as the sea. Given to her by the love she left behind, her human mate." Lafitte leaned forward, his eyes gleaming. "It was no small gem, mylady, and worth more than most lives."

"What does a ghost pirate do with money?" The question was

out of my mouth before I could stop it, but to my relief Lafitte dipped his head back to laugh.

"Fair question, indeed. It's not about its worth for resale, mistress. For one such as myself, who's lived many lives and amassed many treasures, 'tis about the ownership. Nothing more."

There were still dozens of pieces of furniture tucked away in storage and crevices of the house I hadn't inspected. It could be in there, hidden somewhere only she knew. Her silence when I'd asked what Lafitte was looking for came back to me.

"You think she's hiding it." At his lifted eyebrow, I clarified. "Bridge House. You think she's keeping it from you."

"Aye and I wouldn't put it past her as she's a willful lass." Lafitte templed his fingers, an awkward gesture given he was balancing himself in a tiny boat. "Lucas convinced me Talia had skirted it off the island, and I was fool enough to believe him. No doubt he knew I'd return to confront him, though by then he'd have the power of North Bridge at his fingertips. 'Twas pure luck for him the bridge's magic faded, and we were unable to return."

That got me. Dimitri had power now? I knew he had a connection to North Bridge, but I'd assumed it was similar to what I felt for the island. He'd run so hot and cold since he'd claimed the bridge ... was he struggling to manage that power? And did he need it to help me keep the island safe?

His fear of Lafitte suddenly made sense. It wasn't just that Lafitte had whisked him away. Lafitte's return meant confronting Lucas's many betrayals, and I had no doubt there were many. I glanced beyond North Bridge, where the water opened to the rest of the world, with a shudder.

Now that we were welcoming the supernatural back to Bridge Island, more than just the ones in need would be arriving. I'd have to be prepared. And I'd need allies. A massive ghost pirate crew seemed like a good start.

"Jean Lafitte, privateer and diplomat, as mistress of Bridge House, I pledge to you this: I will seek out Talia's Star and give it to you. Though it belongs to the island, I will honor the bargain Lucas made in my absence. And I will trust you to protect and care for it for ... well ... I guess eternity."

He cocked his head to one side, stroking his chin like a cartoon villain.

"And in return? What is it the guardian of Bridge Island wants?"

"I want you and your crew to leave today. Without animosity, but with the understanding that I'm rebuilding something here that was neglected for far too long. I want the space to do that without additional complications."

"Like a crew of pirates with bewitched rum, mylady?"

"Exactly," I replied to the one-armed man, who'd apparently decided it was time to contribute to the conversation. "A smooth re-opening, a chance to find my footing in my new responsibilities, and time to convince Bridge House to tell me where Talia's Star is hidden."

I lifted my hand to Lafitte again.

"I need us to work together, Lafitte. I'm much better at looking forward when I don't have to glance over my shoulder. And something tells me I'll need your help again."

His mustache lifted with his grin, and I knew I had him. Jean Lafitte couldn't resist a good bargain, or a damsel in distress. He gripped my hand in both of his and shook.

"We have a pact, Misty of Bridge House. The crew and I will set sail today."

True to his word, Jean Lafitte and his crew of mystical misfits pulled up their anchor and drifted away from Bridge Island as the sun set that evening. I watched from the balcony as they passed through North Bridge and faded away, Lafitte waving goodbye with that same devilish grin until he disappeared beyond the bayou.

CHAPTER 15

Kitty was at the foot of the stairs with a mug of hot coffee the next morning when I came down after a restful night. I took it into the sitting room, where we'd added a desk we could use as a check-in station. One of the shelves had been cleared of baubles, and Pop's picture frames were on display. There was a small plaque explaining why they were special, because it wasn't obvious to the naked eye, and a pricelist.

I'd be surprised if we sold a single one. But that wasn't why they were there. Not really.

A bloom of roses in the window beckoned me to bury my nose in them. The vase was polished gold, shined so deep I could see my reflection. A little flutter danced across my pulse.

"Ready for the big day, boss?" Max's hair was freshly washed and perfectly parted. His clean, trimmed nails lifted to his ears for a good scratch, but he caught them midway and shoved his hands in his pocket. He seemed to be handling the werewolf thing pretty well. But we still had a flea problem to contend with.

I gave him a fist bump.

"Let's do this, groundskeeper Max."

I don't know what I'd expected, but the constant barrage of people coming in and out was not it. Well-wishers from New

Orleans and Treater's Way came by to tour the grounds and see the refurbished house. Guests checked in and dashed up to their rooms. The cafe patrons overflowed to the porch, munching on bowls of candy we put out.

I let my intuition tell me where to go. Who to greet. When to linger. A dragon I'd briefly met when I first came to the island pulled me into a hard hug before accidentally stepping on my toes. The fairy-leader of a frolic from Baton Rouge presented me with a bottle of nectar that every sense I had told me never to drink. The supreme from a coven in Mississippi performed a protection ceremony on the path leading to the house.

I thanked them all and appreciated the show of support from a supernatural community I knew very little about. But my attention was drawn to the stumbling centaur who asked if we had a stable and the young griffin staring at the treetops. They were the ones I was meant to focus on, their shaky silhouettes telling me they had no idea what they were capable of.

I couldn't wait to show them.

By the time the sun set, my feet ached, and my stomach rumbled. I dropped into a chair at the cafe with an appreciative groan. Kitty set a tray in front of me. A bowl of pumpkin soup, crusty bread, and iced water with lemon. I whimpered in appreciation.

"This is exactly what I wanted."

"Yeah, no kidding." Kitty rolled her eyes, but with less vigor than usual, and she bumped me with her hip as she went back into the kitchen to help Sam clean up. Iris joined me at the table, reaching one hand toward my bread. I growled.

"Fair enough. You've earned the entire loaf," she said with a laugh. I broke a chunk off and handed it to my bestie.

"Couldn't have gotten here without you."

We chatted about the day while I ate. Kitty reappeared with wine—legit, not fairy or pirate she promised—and Iris and I toasted the new season.

"You did great today." She swirled the glass, holding it up to the light to watch the colors deepen. "I thought you'd need more guidance, but every time I checked on you, you were right where you needed to be."

"I finally figured it out, Iris. It's just about meeting people where they are. I've always been good at that part." I let the wine sit on my tongue, enjoying the hint of pepper, enjoying the deep satisfaction in my bones. I dipped the glass in her direction. "Of course, I didn't get here alone."

"Well, I do what I can." She tossed her hair over one shoulder with a grin. "The roses in the sitting room are lovely."

"Dimitri left them for me. At least I think he did. The vase reminds me of him."

Iris was silent for a moment, her gaze drifting toward the water, her eyes just a touch sad.

"He's done great, too."

"Hey, Iris." I squeezed her hand, waiting until she turned back to me. "Everyone on the island gets a second chance. That's what we're about."

We shared a smile, then raised another cheers with our wine, just because we could.

73

CHAPTER 16

*T*he sun was down, the ship was gone, my stomach was full, and my guests had settled.

My guests. The Bridge House had guests. Some supernatural and others along for the ride. When I closed my eyes, I could sense their energies. I would be able to tell, I realized, when one was ready to transition or if another was fighting their nature. I would read their turmoil like a book. And I'd be able to help them.

Probably not all of them. Life wasn't that smooth. But I had something to offer. A purpose beyond being a wife and mother. Not that those were bad things. But this ... this was uniquely mine. It filled my soul. As unusual and beautiful as my mermaid's tail.

My siren hummed in delight, begging for a night swim, and I was ready to oblige.

Norbert wasn't at his perch, but that was okay. I had a different destination tonight. I wrapped my clothes in a tight plastic bag and tied it around my wrist. Even knowing Dimitri had stashed them all over the island for me, a gesture that still gave me butterflies, I wanted to be safe.

Then, instead of wading in, I dove.

I circled the island, gliding past deep rock formations I'd never noticed before, like the remnants of a long-dormant volcano. There were large patches of moss, brilliant and green under the night sky, and fish that swam alongside me, curious and playful, while others watched warily from the security of their coves. I waved like a goofball, as if they could understand such a human gesture.

It didn't matter. Even under water part of me kept my humanity. Just like above the surface I had a tail.

When the moon was tall overhead, I swam to my destination, waiting naked on the shore until I was dry enough to put my clothes on. Then I tiptoed over to Dimitri's cabin and knocked on the door.

Sleep still put a fog in his lovely golden eyes when he answered. A hint of stubble lined his square jaw. His shirt was wrinkled, and his pillow had left a slight red line along his cheek that I wanted to run my hand across.

Still, he smiled as if happy to see me.

"How was the grand opening?"

"Perfect." I leaned against the doorway, bringing myself closer to him. My fingers itched to touch him. I let them follow the smooth lines of his biceps, enjoying how his eyes swirled like lava, all sleep gone. "I got your flowers."

"I'm glad." A hint of sheepishness cast a blush across his neck that radiated heat deep into my core. I breathed it in, slow and steady.

"I wanted to tell you something. I figured out what I want to be called. You know, instead of mistress."

"Not queen?" His smile widened.

"Definitely not," I laughed. My fingers trailed down his arm, then I wrapped his hand in mine and squeezed. "I've landed on caretaker. That's who I am. That's what I do." I brought his hand to my lips, rotated it, and planted a small kiss on his palm. "I was born to take care of things and people. I think it fits perfectly."

His pinkie caressed my cheek. We'd been here before, not that long ago. At the time, he'd turned away from me. And I hadn't been ready.

But everything was different now.

I raised to the tips of my toes, bringing our eyes level, drawing his hand to my waist. A happy sigh escaped me as he pressed his fingers into my skin.

Dimitri dipped his head down.

I lifted my chin up.

I couldn't remember my last first kiss. I expected nerves. But for once, my brain was quiet. I wasn't worried about whether I would do it right or if my lips were too chapped or if I still tasted of the bayou.

I just wanted Dimitri.

Our lips met, feather light and full of sparks that set all the tiny hairs on my skin alight. It was tentative. The kiss of two friends who knew that this moment changed everything.

For the first time in my life, change didn't scare me. Not one bit.

I pressed myself closer to his chest. His arm circled me.

When our lips met the second time, there was nothing light about it. There was nothing tentative or unsure. The force of it sent a bolt of lightning through me. His hands, tender only moments ago, dug into my back in a way that made me scream for more.

I was full of his scent. The odd combination of diesel fuel and cedarwood that somehow I'd come to enjoy. His stubble grazed my skin, the promise of something not quite soft but not quite rough. He hummed in the back of his throat, like a finely tuned engine purring.

I broke away to catch my breath, my lips raw, my heart pounding.

"Caretaker." One corner of his mouth lifted into a sly grin I'd never seen before. A different kind of gruffness filled his voice.

Not the grumpy troll. The husk of a man who knew what he wanted. My hot, gruff, golden troll ... so full of surprises. "It suits you."

I brushed alongside him, letting myself into his cabin.

"So do you."

All Hallows' Eve was nearly over. Bridge House was content. North Bridge was at full power. The island was in harmony.

And I was ready for a treat.

Dimitri pulled me close, closing the door behind us.

It's THE HOLIDAY SEASON, and the island is feeling festive. Except Misty, who's a major grinch until three unexpected visits put her in full scrooge mode .. especially when she swims into a vision of her future.

^^^ Scan the code above or click here to start reading the festively final fifth book *Bridge Over Seasoned Water*.

WHEN A CLUMSY DRAGON turns out to be her scorching hot ex, will an independent therapist reignite an old spark or let it smother?

Get The Ebook

^^^ Scan the code above or click here to claim your copy of *Not Yet Old Flames* when you join my newsletter.

ACKNOWLEDGMENTS

This one's for all the women out there who have a pirate's spirit and always dive in to the deep end. Find out what happiness feels like. You deserve it.

ABOUT JB LASSALLE

JB (Jen) Lassalle is a writer of later-in-life fantasy and low-steam romantic fantasy. She likes strong females, dimensional males, and found family friendships that triumph over nuanced bad guys you love to hate.

Jen is a New Orleans resident. The city, and the surrounding areas, serve as a rich backdrop for a world where magic exists and mystical creatures are not only real, but live among us.

When Jen isn't writing, she's hanging with her family and friends at a local park or coffee shop. She likes working out, which is kind of weird, loves yoga, and plays video games. Of course, she reads.

Jen and her husband have two kids. One is an avid competitive swimmer (which sucks up all their weekend time). The other is a daydreamer like Jen who plays the Mega Man theme on his guitar and kicks around a soccer ball.

Jen isn't great with social media, but you can connect with her below. Or, join her newsletter when you claim your copy of *Not Yet Old Flames,* a second-chance PWF romantic short.

facebook.com/jblassalle

instagram.com/jblassalle

amazon.com/JB-Lassalle/e/B0BFJXP4GC

Made in United States
Troutdale, OR
11/24/2024

25186725R00053